J.C. Signaturework...

PRESENTS

A P R I L
"THE BOOK OF VICTORY"

APRIL

"THE BOOK OF VICTORY"

April, The Book of Victory
Copyright © 2010 by Joe Calloway

ISBN: 978-1-4507-1506-5

Published by Joe Calloway
for J.C. Signatureworks 2010

Edited by Kruti Calloway
for KayJay & Associates, LLP

10 9 8 7 6 5 4 3 2 1 0

Printed in the U.S.A.

J.C. Signatureworks PRESENT

APRIL
"THE BOOK OF VICTORY"

A 2010 COLLECTION OF POETRY

Forward

It is procrastination that keeps people from truly succeeding in most endeavors. You could have a really great idea, but until you put effort, consistency, hope and belief behind what you seek to accomplish, time will just pass you by.

Understand this law, TIME WILL NOT STOP. Even I had become tiresome of the phrase, "I'll get to it later". Almost 11 years went by before I produced my first sub-novelty. The first poetry book I wrote was done in a week.

I know I have this gift to write, whether it's a novelty or just a poetry book, all I have to do is what was stated earlier. The plan of this year, book wise, is to produce one poetry book per month.

I'm not sure if this is going to be about making dollars, but what is certain is that it will be about the ability to produce. This is my desire. This is my task. This is…"THE BOOK OF VICTORY" and there's still more to conquer.

The Book of Victory

-

*You will have trials, you will fall
short of some things, but stay
strong and faithful and you will
be victorious*

God has brought me through all of my life's obstacles and this book was written as a testimony and an encouragement to you. Be victorious today.

Table of Contents

iv

Intro: A.M.O.W.

A Moment of Worship to my Lord and King
For His love and mercy, are such a powerful thing
To understand that His breath allows me to breathe
For every time I ran out, He still didn't leave
Never cursing the father, but sinning to death
Gotta live at the altar to deal with the flesh
It wants nothing better than hell in high water
So I load up on prayer to restore some order
Read a few chapters, like Matthew, Mark, John,
Deuteronomy, Leviticus, Proverbs and Psalms
The word have I hid in my heart, yet it is still corrupt
I just keep pressing on, I won't give up
I've seen what can occur, when the righteous pray
You could plan for tomorrow, but make today
The best it can be, amidst the storm
Remember when Jesus spoke, peace be calm
No, peace be still and it all went silent
Why do things of this earth get so violent?
Earthquakes and tornados, volcanoes and fire
People loosing their homes, money down to the wire
Pay cuts and job losses, economic stress
To those who are believers, it's such a big mess
And to wanna go on, it might seem crazy
To wanna leave church, you're out your mind baby
What you need is a little more time and A.M.O.W.

Although You Fell

Whenever you start working on a plan
Things get thrown in the way
It seems hard to stand
Your focus gets fought on every end
Distraction after distraction
Just gone with the wind
You know you can do it
It's not a question of how
You just think to yourself, will time allow?
You pray and you fast
Then you're fast asleep
But with every passing minute
You're not counting sheep
You're asking for forgiveness
Hearing God speak clearly
So that when you rise in the morning
You have a testimony to share
You battled with cancer for 8 long years
And in the midst of the 9th
You stopped shedding tears
You got your life right, now living well
You stood on God's word, although you fell
Got that phone call, with victory news
Shouting no more cancer, no more blues
Hallelujah to the Lord Almighty

Hey Momma

Hey Momma, if you read this, please understand
I'm writing about victory, so raise your hand
Like a boxer after a bout, the winner is
You, because Mom, you did well with your kids
I'm going to talk about the past
It's not to bring you down
But to celebrate in the difference, of where you are now
There were trials in your life
Some great and some small
Some involving drugs, abuse and alcohol
Birthdays, Christmas, special holidays
In spite of all the mess
They were the best in a lot of ways
I look back on it now and I remember this
No matter how bad it got
You ruled with an iron fist
You made it your business, to see us do well
And I'm proud of you mom
Because all of us fail
At some point in our life, a storm gets goin'
Loss of money, track of time, stress levels showin'
I look at your progress in two thousand and ten
Writing to my readers, these battles you can win
Hey Momma if you're reading this, this one thing is true
That if nobody else in the world does, I believe in you

Wounded Soldier

Looking at the numbers and the odds of winning
You go in seeing the struggle, not thinking of the ending
What's crazy is that you know, only two things are real
In a warring situation, is to kill or be killed
There could be days of planning, lookin' for the unknown
But in the heat of that battle, there's a change of tone
The momentum keeps shifting, from the rugged and rough
To the ones well prepared, being mentally tough
In my life, I've had battles I just knew I would lose
Until I realized, that winning was something to choose
It all came down to being prepared
Even for the unexpected things I feared
I look at war films and how they portray to me
Life and death in the middle, it amazes me
That some don't even value that, they just grow psychotic
Trying to hurt everything breathin' and don't care about it
I was faced with situations, I'm glad I got through
Can't imagine what it would be like or what I would do
If my heart would keep humble or bubble and bust
If at the end of the day, it was someone I could trust
They say, go down swinging, do your best in the fight
If it were really bad news, could you sleep at night
War aint no joke, for a country or self
For family, for establishment and everything else
If you live through it, you're just a wounded soldier

The Straight & Narrow

The path to destruction is broad and wide
But the path to righteousness, is like stay inside
There's no room to go, to the left or the right
And at the end of this tunnel is a really small light
So you just have to trust and stay on the path
Curvin' a little bit, can ruin the task
The broad has room for error, there's so much space
Good luck though, trying to get to the designated place
This road isn't for everyone, so please form a line
There's no side by side walkin' and death is the fine
For unruly characteristics or sadistic thinking
For worshipping idols or lustful eye-winking
For lying or cheating, murder or theft
For fornication or adultery or whatever is left
The straight and the narrow, like an arrow and bow
Pointed in one direction, to which it must go
The law and the purpose, will surface in time
We will all stand before Him, like a judge to a crime
The prosecutor and the jury, the judge and the bailiff
All wrapped in one, to see your life unveileth
As much as you try, you're gonna fall down
Just don't sit there and cry, keep moving now
Ask to be strengthened and work on your faults
And destroy all your secrets and misguiding vaults
Go tell someone, His eye is on the sparrow
And whatever you do, stay on the straight and narrow

Camp Haluwasa

You may ask, what's so special about this place
Well it's a Christian Camp and where I saw God's face
Not in the manner of which you might speculate
More like the burning bush for Moses
Or seeing a talking milk crate
Something unusual, something hard to explain
Something you just can't get, to simplify in your brain
Well in this moment of visitation, two things changed
What I thought about God and what I felt was strange
There were a couple of teens there, adults and youth
We had a couple of open sessions, to speak of the truth
The truth being Jesus, who is the Word
The way and the light, haven't you heard?
That all things are possible, words from the Holy book
I was singing a song and my whole body shook
Got up early that morning and took a walk alone
I remember reading a scripture
That said God came off the throne
To come to the aid of His servant
Like every governing body, wrapped in a surgeon
To heal and to rescue, to give strength and support
To bring a feeling of triumph, like the final award in a sport
I was tired and stressed out, asking why Lord me?
I believe at Camp Haluwasa, is where I was set free
So no matter the challenges, I will have the victory

Out There

I was asked this question...
Do you have that many poems in you?
I'd figured, after 33 years of life
I could begin to
Talk about what I've seen, in others and in me
At home, school and work, even ministry
Peoples' flaws and strengths
Some of their great ideas
Even in some sad defeats, I still said cheers
Why? I look at the knowledge
I've obtained in each one
And with every new day granted
I state my life has begun
To grow stronger and better
Because of the decisions I make
Some of them good for the most
Some seem like a mistake
Somewhere out there
Where sky meets water
Is where I keep looking, because there is order
A perspective of perfection
When you're surrounded by dirt
Chaos, misguidance, corruption and hurt
Out there in a distance, where the answers are
You must travel by faith, not with a car

Promise

They say that promises are made to be broken
Then why even make them, if you're simply just jokin'?
In a way, that's what you're saying
Just entertaining my dreams
And every self motivation I have, it seems
That a promise is like something borrowed
You might get it back
If it comes back tomorrow, that is great jack
But what happens when what I promise is years overdue?
Let go or keep believing, that it will eventually come true
I've had many promises spoken to me
Some took a little while, some I'm still hopin' to see
You could get caught up sometimes
On the idea that it's wrapped with a bow
But it could have come and gone and you wouldn't know
Promises, promises, big or small
You may be given just one and someone else given all
I remember getting jealous when I saw this occur
Now whatever was promised after, to me, was a blur
I couldn't even see it, which left me to believe
These promises, promises, I would never achieve
Then one day I recapped and saw real clear
That all of my promises, were sitting right there
They needed me to open them, be them and live
To also realize, that they were here for me to give...to you

In His Hands

It's just something about prayer
When you're going through
Melodies of music and Psalm
When you don't know what to do
When your faith is being tested
Even your love for Christ
Trying to understand His sacrifice
Warring with your mind, your spirit and soul
Feeling overwhelmed, no longer a whole
Broken into pieces, you just cry hard
Thinking about a movie, live free or die hard
Wondering why Jehovah, hasn't heard you say
The things you have need of, each time you pray
You start thinkin' to yourself
Before Him, things weren't this bad
These current situations
Weren't like the previous ones you had
They seem a lot deeper, more intense and such
A heavy load on you now, you cry, "it's too much"
You hear some words of encouragement
Something unusual to do
Sow a seed of expectancy to get through this too
Because of your walk, you heed His commands
And testify that, this time
You were in His hands

The Book of Victory

The book of victory, can I just be plain?
Writing each month, is really a strain
It's easy to just talk and say line to line
What comes from the heart or what's on my mind
It's when I have to produce a poem each day
And strategize on the layout and the things I say
So, I get to this poem or chapter if you will
And see the vision clearly, peace be still
The mind has to do more, in the work I create
To accomplish this goal and make something great
With each book that I'm writing, I notice this pattern
Page nine is the title hook, the light in the lantern
The reminder of the book that my readers are reading
A reminder to self that I am proceeding
To discipline myself to stay full throttle
Like an addict who makes sure to put down the bottle
How else will he overcome, except day by day
Fighting his demons, clearing the way
For soberness and health and things he has lost
Because in the beginning, he didn't count the cost
The book of victory is about the struggles and trials
And achieving little by little, through frowns and smiles
You gotta stop looking at the struggle, being so quickly
Defeated by it's presence, eventually
The war will be over, try seeing the victory

What'chu Want?

Book number five and many more to go
With all these thoughts in my head
You'd think they'd just flow
Right out of my mental, onto this paper
Like a camera flashin' pictures of a nice skyscraper
Well it's become harder
I get brain freeze sometimes
I guess, because I'm stuck on everything rhymes
Configuration like PC, same I.P. address
Trying to ping my own network, left with stress
Or messages of failure, I tell ya no lie
At times I wanna quit and the reason why...
It gets overwhelming to know where I am
Having fun on the river, until I get to the dam
Seeing the cut-off point, turn back or just fall?
Believe you'll survive or don't go at all
I'm faced with this challenge, to write 11 books
With various concepts and various looks
You ever get an assignment, you knew was a trip?
You get started on it, then time cracks the whip
You hope time slows up and a second is a minute
Just enough stalling to help you get in it
Well I'ma be strong, you do the same, don't front
Because it's not what you have, but what you want
In order to get there, you gotta keep pressin'

The Enemy

There's light and darkness, there's good and bad
There's times when I'm happy and times when I'm sad
This Yen and Yang concept that surrounds mankind
Plays on the emotions of the heart and mind
The nature of a person that loves and hates
Wanting to be perfect, mistake after mistake
Selfish and giving, kind and angry
Beautiful like doves, then like dogs that are mangy
So many ups in downs in the ways we portray
Saying good morning to a neighbor and still have a bad day
Well let me tell you a lil' something, you may already know
There is a spiritual enemy, yes an unseen foe
He rules this system of things, the opposite of God
He pursues and persuades with a devilish rod
Not that rod of correction, that makes you do right
But the one that causes treason and nations to fight
For wars to be broadcasted wherever there is peace
For love to be discontinued and for prayer to cease
For the connection of man to his father in heaven
Broken and destroyed, separating the brethren
Who believe and speak proudly of their life with Christ
This enemy unseen, he doesn't play nice
He causes disruption in families and friends
Breaking focus and prosperity, reminding us of sins
Just tell him everyday, that in the end, the believer wins

The Job Experience

The Job experience, read Job chapter 1
Why is everything so biblical?
You'll understand when I'm done
Satan got permission to test the servant Job
If this was one of us, like a bomb, we'd explode
We couldn't handle such pain, deception and lack
We couldn't deal with the idea
Of what might never come back
Job was blameless and upright
Had seven sons and three daughters
Had plenty of what he needed like streaming waters
Everything flowed in it's assignment
Let's just say he was blessed
Then it was taken away
Job became stressed
Friends came talking, like what God do you serve?
That he would let you lose everything?
Almost your nerve?
To question the father on what purpose he had
To the point, you stop believing, grow weary and mad
Job took of his robe and start praising the Lord
One bad message after another
His servants dying by the sword
His entire family gone in a day
Cursed to the point of death and never did he say...

Through The Fire

You will be tested one day
When you truly stand for something real
When you decide to keep pressin'
Even when your wounds don't heal
Fight after fight, one let down after another
So many promises broken, can't count on a brother
Dreams becoming nightmares
Because the truth came out
And everything you had hope for
You stop thinkin' about
You get on the same page as the wild and corrupt
Try living like they do, but something stirs in your gut
You fight with your inner man on why this is good
But the spirit keeps tuggin' and you know what you should
Do in the morning and do every night
What should be on your mind, when temptation's in sight
What words you should be speaking
When doubt comes around
Because whatever you did in the past
Might not work for you now
You get thrown in the fire, like the faithful three
But you don't bow down to captivity
You got more motivated with Christ in the midst
Start praying a little harder, I'm gonna get through this
Then you came out, unharmed and unburned

In The Den

It's just another level of your faithfulness
When you get thrown in the den for another test
Let's bring this story to our time
You're with a group of friends
Talking about the girls and getting some skins
The street terminology for getting some sex
Knowing how to get there and what to do next
But amongst this young crowd
Is a Christian soul
Who likes to be on his best behavior
And do what he's told
For all of his obedience, his rewards are great
Then one day he decides, he could come home late
He's not planning to be reckless or do something strange
But with the direction he's going
This situation will change
Too good for his own good, he's brought to a place
Where every bad thing is good, just sample a taste
He knows he shouldn't be there
But his only out, is sin
And this is where, the real challenge begins
Do you give in to the lust or power your will?
Remembering who you are, saying peace be still
You keep your mind focused, for this one thing to win
That's spirit over flesh, when you're thrown in the den

Pit To The Palace

The first thing you do with this topic
Is put it in a natural sense
Like going from jail to the White House
Yeah, now that's suspense
But let me take you a different route
Have you try something new
Like, understanding that one day
This flesh will be taken away from you
Our spirit is in a pit, we try hard to make neat
By going to church, being nice and stayin' out the street
I mean, a lot more is involved
You have to do these things daily
Keep your mind right, pray everyday
Feed your heart and your belly
Because when the natural part of you
That part we can touch
Returns to the earth in the form of dust
The part of you that's your senses
Will return to the creator
So from this pit to the heavens, there's no place greater
Now typically you'd think to be locked in a cell
And the palace to you, would be something upscale
Like a nice home or apartment, mansion or loft
Just remember what I said if you seem to get lost
The pit to the palace, is more like earth to heaven

While You Wait

Now understand, while you wait
Don't let life pass you by
We all have a purpose to fulfill
Most times, the reason why
We never get going in the life that was designed
Is because when the offer was made
Most of us just declined
To accept our real purpose, so we do whatever
It works for a while, then comes stormy weather
Things to try our patience, make us go nuts
Costing people their lives or a million bucks
Not a million per say, but you get my drift
Sometimes while you wait, you might need a lift
A lift in your spirit, to get you through
Some words of wisdom, help you decide what to do
Most times we battle ourselves, to even give a rip
A nice way of saying, not caring, before we slip
Good part about falling is, if you can get up
Then you're getting better at walking, it's not luck
God is overseeing the path and the rocks
The dirt that gets on you, those building blocks
We like to call problems and turn back around
Or just settling for less, cause that's easy now
Power up your ambition, give chase to the bait
You're destined to succeed, but while you wait...

The Great Escape

...prepare for the great escape, the Lord has given you
I know it seems like I'm saying the same thing
At times I do, but it's all in the ministering
And stirring of gifts, for days when
You're on your P's and Q's and there's changing shifts
See, the enemy won't rest, he'll do the same thing twice
You'll ignore it at first, but then it'll look nice
You'll be like oh yeah, now that's the stuff
Then a minute day later, your life gets rough
Work says you're fired, we're laying you off
Child in the hospital with a serious cough
Near death experience, you cry and complain
As if that wasn't enough, got a migraine
Young people on the block, outside playing loud
Then an argument starts, gun shots in the crowd
And you think to yourself, oh my God, lil' Jeff
Go running outside, you have no nerve left
So carelessly running, one thing on your mind
That in this crowd full of people, you don't find
Little Jeffery there bleeding, saying daddy ouch
You were sleeping this whole time, son right on the couch
Singing Jesus loves me, this I know
For the bible tells me so
You look in his eyes as if watching a tape
Thanking Jehovah Jireh for the great escape

Sanctuary

This is the place where all saints meet
To give praise to Jehovah for one more defeat
All through the week, getting pushed around
Testifying to the song, we fall down
But if you need a little stitching
Some patches and glue
Some healing in your body, this is the place for you
There's hospitals and clinics, that's available too
Some things happen here, that Docs can't do
Like provide spiritual healing, give rest to the soul
Give wisdom and guidance to a short-term goal
Something you know isn't possible
The natural laws aren't compliant
So if you can't believe in God
You rely on science and modern technology
Biology and pills and anything that get's you goin'
Like brand new wheels
I'm here to let you know
There's something about this place
That when you eat of it's fruit
You keep needing that taste
It's not always the music or united sound
It's not in your voice being lost, but in all you found
The strength and the peace to go out again
Facing your battles and knowing you'll win. Amen

The Secret Place

Now it doesn't stop there, if you seek His face
Sometimes you gotta do this, in the secret place
The secret place is a place, you set aside or assign
To pray to the father, say what's on your mind
You speak like you speak to a loved one or friend
But recognizing His authority as beginning and end
You start by acknowledging his power
Giving thanks for His love, His mercy and forgiveness
Coming down like a dove
Pleasant and beautiful, tried and true
In the secret place, he deals directly with you
Confronts you on mishaps, to straighten you out
Like a dad would do his son, know what I'm talkin' bout?
It's all done in love, because he knows
The first enemy is ourselves and then our foes
So He corrects us gently, with power and might
If this was back in the day, we'd be gone by night
It'd be Sodom and Gomorra, ten plagues and man
Forget havin' a Moses, there'd be no Jordan
We would stay in the wilderness and hope for bread
Man the way we act today, we'd all be dead
So I go to the secret place, confess who I am
He understands I need help and the blood of the Lamb
To wash and forgive, to heal and instill
Not only what I need for myself, but His purpose and will

Peace, Be Still

I remember hearing the story
About the disciples on the boat
Since we're going on a journey
Let me get my coat
Something about faith dictates where you are
And whether or not if in this life you'll get far
Because if you have no faith, trust or hope
Basically your life is hanging by a very thin rope
Faith can give you patience
Faith can give you rest
Faith can take your worst and make it your best
Faith is what allowed Peter to walk
On water that is, so him and Jesus could talk
But before that occurred, a storm arose
The disciples were trippin', Jesus had his eyes closed
Tryina' catch up on some sleep, but was called to come
And to do what he does, make violence numb
Cause chaos to shut up, peace be still
For none of these things are in God's will
From Jonah and the whale to Noah's Ark
The covenant is simple, like a piece of tree bark
Whatever He speaks to, must do what it's told
Jesus is the word, type that in bold
So if you're storm get's all crazy or your mind get's ill
Do what Jesus did, say peace be still

What's Your Goliath

Don't sit there with your army and think you can't win
Don't defeat yourself without seeing the end
The first trap to losing, is losing your place
Forgetting who you are in time and space
You've become a chosen warrior, get ready, get set
Your enemy has lost, just hasn't occurred yet
You think that your losin', cause you're bruisin' so fast
Thinkin' to yourself, how long will it last?
Does God not see my life being torn apart?
He's already seen the end, so seek his heart
Try to understand each battle and war
Although stuck in the middle, winning for sure
But what's your Goliath, what has you shook
That every time it comes around, you can't look?
What's eating at your faith, to make you say
I can't take this no more, not today?
I see you with your sword, your helmet and shield
But because it's so huge, you stay off the field
Got the enemy laughin', teasin' and tauntin'
Gotcha' head under covers, like your house is hauntin'
What's your Goliath, that you can't come forth
Speaking thus sayeth the Lord and change it's course?
Are you scared for your life or just don't have one?
Are you saying after the first hit, ouch, I'm done?
You can win this one too, go read that bible verse
I'm more than a conqueror and strike your enemy first

Strategy

If there's a battle you have, on a daily basis
And the only thing that changes, is the places and faces
Then it's time for a strategy, a simple adjust
Like a change in direction or plan if you must
I find myself doing things that irritate my boo
Because of a life that was established before "I do"
Making plans to get better, adapt and change
Waking up each morning, with a feeling that's strange
Maturing to be a good dad, provide for lil' man
While balancing out the married life's original plan
The house, car and baby and steady careers
With debts to the ceiling, bringing four eyes to tears
Leaning on one another as a couple should
With Jesus as the foundation, so everything's good
We go back and forth about what to do next
With a list full of boxes, but not enough cheques
So we put in a plan, to do small then large
Giving one another authority, to be in charge
If there's lack on my part, she's got my back
And when she can't come through, I pick up the slack
Deeper and deeper the debt might get
But as long as we strategize in the time that's set
All things become possible to them that believe
And the heavenly father, has seen us achieve
So what to do now, is go intercede...*for those in need*

If You're Listening

If you're listening, stop talking, you'll hear a lot clear
The truth of what's happening, this season, this year
What matters now is that you grow and change lives
Cutting through darkness with your spiritual knives
If you're listening, God's watching, watch what you do
Be prepared by the word, when battle comes to you
The adversary is real, he uses all he can
Family and friends, the one you thought was your man
Til' you came one day knockin' and she answered the door
It's the reason why she didn't get you at quarter to four
Your son knew all along, but was told not to speak
Since the argument Friday, he's been creepin' all week
Part of you wants to slap her, kick him in the butt
Pop your son in the head, but you say, "know what?"
Go ahead, keep that life, I'm better than this
You're hurt, feelin' broken, you hope, pray and wish
That one day he wakes up and opens his eyes
Gets his life right and stops telling lies
You ask the Lord for some guidance, to keep you from sin
While your hand pours a glass of that juice and gin
You take down a sip and push it aside
Cause you know that some time ago, he patiently tried
To get you to see then, the things you did
How you treated this man, before your kid
You pray for forgiveness and healing for all
If you're listening, it's Him, will you take the call?

W.A.R.

Worship and Repentance, the duo indeed
Hand in hand in battle, they help you succeed
See a prideful heart, that says I do all
Will separate you from the father, as you continue to fall
Look at Satan's situation, he was a living jewel
Too much pride in his heart, he wanted to rule
Thinkin' he was better than Jehovah and even Christ
Instead of Worship and Repentance, he lost his life
Was hurled to the earth, like a burning rocket
From a pool master who says, "eight ball, corner pocket"
That ended the game, Satan thought he could win
If you have a prideful heart, get rid of it friend
Humble yourself, you're still number one
And the process He's taking you through, is not yet done
Like the carpenter or ironsmith, making a sword
Is sharpening your rough edges, praise the Lord
I know this whole book was written
Giving thanks and praise, because
I realized without him, there'd be no more days
My life could have been over 20 years ago
From the stupid things I did, just trying to make doe
Or by a girl, if not sane enough to put the knife down
Playing over worthless treasures, like a gold ring - now
Fast forward to the present time, where hard times are sure
You need worship and repentance, cause this is w.a.r.

Revelation

The book of revelation, should be my next book
Listen, grab a bible, let's all take a look
Saint John the Divine, was given this brief
To inform and encourage, all with belief
That the Alpha and Omega, the beginning and end
Which was and is to come, would soon begin
To bring to a close, this system of things
Doing away with earth's leaders, queens and kings
Anything or anybody, that didn't live His command
The last poem of this book, I hope you understand
Things get good sometimes, so good, you can't let go
But if it's not honoring Jehovah, what'chu doin' it fo?
When it's all said and done, he'll have the last say
And all this swag you thought you really had
Is going to be washed away
The beast of this earth and the demons below
Gonna rise up, trying to devour what they can yo!
The victory that we should be seeking
Is over our flesh and tone
Pursuing God and His purpose, that comes from the throne
Don't like what'cha reading, well put the book down
Because everything I did, I can't take back now
So I read Revelation, to get some insight
On what really matters to Him and how to get it right
The day is drawing near and we will all be judged - Selah

PUBLICATIONS

JOE CALLOWAY, SR

A BLUE DENIM PUBLICATION

1020 CAMBRIDGE:
The Book Of Dreams
- VOLUME ONE -

A dream is a story that a person watches or appears to take part in
during sleep. Dream events are imaginary, but can be related to real
life events the distance has experienced.

1997-2008

A Semi-Autobiography of the Author's life
and the dreams that have resided with him
even after departing from 1020 Cambridge
Mall in 1997. This book is part of a series,
so stay tuned.

ISBN: 978-1-60585-940-8
Publisher: Blue Denim Publications
Copyright © 2008 Joe Calloway

PUBLICATIONS

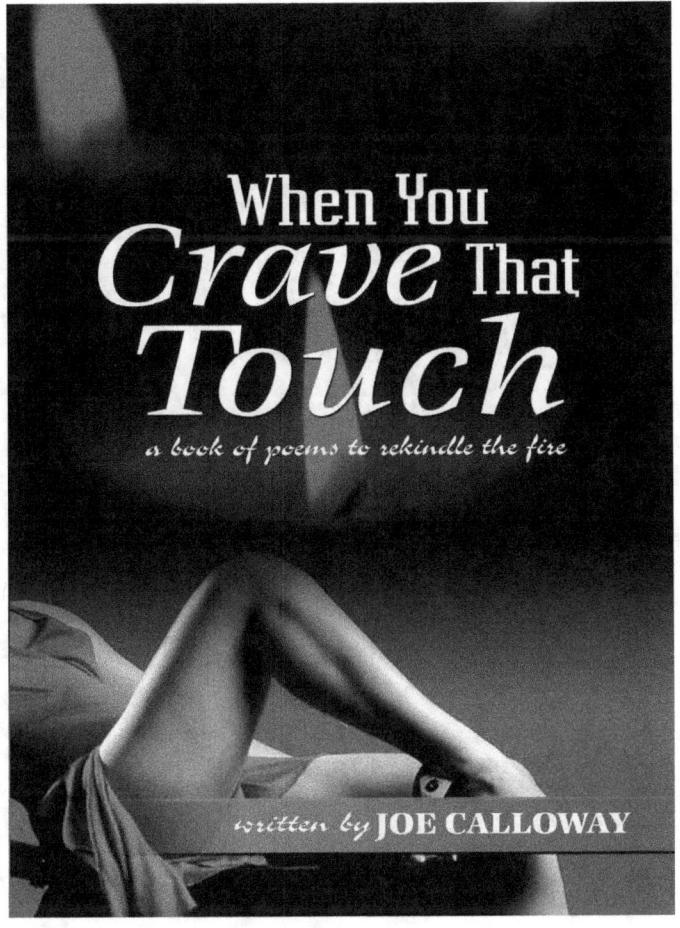

30 uniquely designed story-based poems,
intended for a mature audience, to rekindle
the fire in their relationship. It's also for
those singles out there who just miss having
that touch.

ISBN: 978-1-60585-939-2
Publisher: Forbidden Fruit Publications
Copyright © 2008 Joe Calloway

PUBLICATIONS

Part of the J.C. Signatureworks 2010 Poetry Collection. "February: The Book of Hearts", speaks about the day to day grind of the mind and how the heart perceives life's challenges.

ISBN: 978-1-4507-1036-7
Publisher: J.C. Signatureworks
Copyright © 2010 Joe Calloway

PUBLICATIONS

Part of the J.C. Signatureworks 2010 Poetry Collection. "March: The Book of Life", is my birthday book and an expression of thanks for 33 years of life, opportunities and provisions to bless others.

ISBN: 978-1-4507-1505-8
Publisher: J.C. Signatureworks
Copyright © 2010 Joe Calloway

PUBLICATIONS

Part of the J.C. Signatureworks 2010 Poetry Collection. "April: The Book of Victory", speaks about going through life's challenges and having the faith to press on and come out victorious.

ISBN: 978-1-4507-1506-5
Publisher: J.C. Signatureworks
Copyright © 2010 Joe Calloway

PUBLICATIONS

MAY
"THE BOOK OF SONGS"
PRODUCED BY J.C. SIGNATUREWORKS

A 2010 COLLECTION OF POETRY

Part of the J.C. Signatureworks 2010 Poetry Collection. "May: The Book of Songs", poetry that sounds like or is derived from genres like Jazz, Rock, Hip-Hop, R&B, New Age, Country, Pop and Gospel.

AVAILABLE JUNE 2010
Publisher: J.C. Signatureworks
Copyright © 2010 Joe Calloway

If you have been encouraged by this publication and would like to support my writing ministry, above what you have already done by purchasing this book, send a "Seed of Victory" made out to

**Clarion Call Worship Center
114 W. Ontario Street
Philadelphia, PA 19140**

Attn: Joe Calloway/Pastor Tonia Holmes-West

Thank You